S.W.I.T.C.H.
SERUM WHICH INSTIGATES TOTAL CELLULAR HIJACK

Other books in the S.W.I.T.C.H. series:

SERUM WHICH INSTIGATES TOTAL CELLULAR HIJACK

Crane Fly Crash

Ali Sparkes

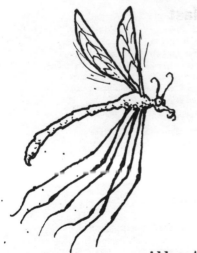

illustrated by
Ross Collins

OXFORD
UNIVERSITY PRESS

OXFORD
UNIVERSITY PRESS

Great Clarendon Street, Oxford OX2 6DP
Oxford University Press is a department of the University of Oxford.
It furthers the University's objective of excellence in research, scholarship,
and education by publishing worldwide in

Oxford   New York

Auckland   Cape Town   Dar es Salaam   Hong Kong   Karachi
Kuala Lumpur   Madrid   Melbourne   Mexico City   Nairobi
New Delhi   Shanghai   Taipei   Toronto

With offices in

Argentina   Austria   Brazil   Chile   Czech Republic   France   Greece
Guatemala   Hungary   Italy   Japan   Poland   Portugal   Singapore
South Korea   Switzerland   Thailand   Turkey   Ukraine   Vietnam

Oxford is a registered trade mark of Oxford University Press
in the UK and in certain other countries

British Library Cataloguing in Publication Data
Data available

ISBN: 978-0-19-2729361
1 3 5 7 9 10 8 6 4 2

Printed in Great Britain

Paper used in the production of this book is a natural,
recyclable product made from wood grown in sustainable forests.
The manufacturing process conforms to the environmental
regulations of the country of origin.

For Freddie Michael

Danny and Josh
(and Piddle)

They might be twins but they're NOT the same! Josh loves insects, spiders, beetles and bugs. Danny can't stand them. Anything little with multiple legs freaks him out. So sharing a bedroom with Josh can be . . . erm . . . interesting. Mind you, they both love putting earwigs in big sister Jenny's pants drawer . . .

Danny

- **FULL NAME:** Danny Phillips
- **AGE:** 8 years
- **HEIGHT:** Taller than Josh
- **FAVOURITE THING:** Skateboarding
- **WORST THING:** Creepy-crawlies and tidying
- **AMBITION:** To be a stunt man

Josh

- FULL NAME: Josh Phillips
- AGE: 8 years
- HEIGHT: Taller than Danny
- FAVOURITE THING: Collecting insects
- WORST THING: Skateboarding
- AMBITION: To be an entomologist

Piddle

- FULL NAME: Piddle the dog Phillips
- AGE: 2 dog years
  (14 in human years)
- HEIGHT: Not very
- FAVOURITE THING: Chasing sticks
- WORST THING: Cats
- AMBITION: To bite a squirrel

CONTENTS

Something In the Hair Tonight

A horrific murder was about to take place in a dark alley. The victim fluttered helplessly in the shadow of a terrifying spiked weapon which pounded against the wall, missing only by inches.

The murderer was cold. Unfeeling. Able to kill with a single blow and then turn away without a moment's remorse. The victim knew time was nearly up. One more attack and there would be nothing left but a mashed corpse.

The spiked weapon swung forward.

'Jenny! Stop it!' Josh leaped across his big sister's bedroom floor and grabbed her arm just before it swung the hairbrush down again.

'Hey! Get off!' yelled Jenny, trying to shake her little brother off her arm. But now his twin,

Danny, came running in too, with an excited whoop, and threw himself at her other arm.

'You're a murderer!' shrieked Josh. 'Killing innocent moths! How could you?'

The poor moth in question flapped limply up the wall from behind Jenny's bed and bumbled against the windowpane, trying to get away.

'It's just a *moth*, Josh! Not a cat or a dog or a person!' snapped Jenny, her long blonde hair whipping about as she wrestled with her brothers.

'Just because it's small, doesn't mean it doesn't have feelings,' said Danny, now climbing onto his sister's back and making her spin round furiously.

'Danny! *Get off*!' Jenny whacked her elbows back, and Danny fell onto her bed. Josh had let his sister go and was now peering closely at the brown moth. Jenny shook her head at Danny. 'You don't even *like* creepy-crawlies. You go nuts if one lands on *you*!'

'True,' shrugged Danny. 'They can be creepy— but they are quite amazing too. I should know. I've been a spider, you know. And a bluebottle. And a grasshopper. Oh—and an ant. That was amazing!'

'Yeah, right,' snorted Jenny. 'Well, you always creep *me* out, anyway!'

Danny laughed. He knew Jenny couldn't possibly believe what he'd just said. Even though it was true. He and Josh *had* been all those creatures over the summer, ever since they stumbled into the secret laboratory in next door's garden and discovered something incredible.

Their neighbour, Petty Potts, might seem like a batty old lady, but it turned out she was a genius scientist who had invented SWITCH—a spray which could turn you into a creepy-crawly. Only Danny and Josh knew her secret since the day when they had accidentally got sprayed and turned into spiders. They'd been afraid of her at first but now they were helping her by searching for some special missing cubes. They'd got four already, but if they found just two more, Petty would have the code to make a new SWITCH spray—which could change you into a reptile. They could find out how it felt to be a snake, or a lizard, or even an alligator!

'You don't *have* to kill him, you know,' Josh told Jenny, still examining the moth. 'All you have to do is open the window.'

'I've tried *that*,' huffed Jenny. 'But it just keeps flying back in!'

'You need to turn your light off,' explained Josh, reaching over and switching off Jenny's bedside lamp. 'Moths get confused and think it's the moon and keep flying towards it.' He eased open the window, blew gently on the moth, and smiled as it flew away into the night. 'Off you go, hawky!' he called after it. 'Go get your tea!' He closed the

window and glanced back into the room where
Danny was squirming on the bed with Jenny's foot
on his head. 'It's a hawk moth. They feed on nectar
by moonlight. Isn't that sweet? And they can smell
their girlfriends from miles and miles away.'

'Eeeuurgh,' commented Danny.

'Yeah, thanks for the biology lesson, you freaky
little bug boffin,' said Jenny, finally releasing Danny
and switching her lamp back on. 'Now get out of
my room, both of you. I've got to get ready to go
out.' And she flounced to her mirror and started
to brush her hair with the deadly weapon, while
rummaging through all the bottles and pots of hair
and make-up stuff. 'MUM!' she bellowed, ignoring
them. 'Where's my hair spray?'

Mum didn't answer—she was singing along to the radio in the kitchen—but the doorbell rang as Josh and Danny mooched out of Jenny's room, and shrugged at each other . . . Jenny was *such* a teenager.

Danny slid down the banister and leaped off at the bottom step, landing with a thud by the front door and opening it a second later.

Standing on the doorstep was Petty Potts. As soon as she saw Danny, and Josh stepping up behind him, she darted her eyes left and right behind her thick spectacles and hissed, 'Excellent! The very people I was hoping for!' Her tweedy old hat was pulled down low over her face and the collar of her old trench coat was turned up. She looked as if she was pretending to be a spy.

'Shhhhhh!' said Petty, not coming into the house but leaning closer to them. 'Now listen—this is very important. Very important.'

'What is?' said Danny.

'Hush! Shhhh!' Petty pulled her coat tight across her chest and frowned at Danny. 'I need your help—but only you two must know!'

Josh sighed. Sometimes he thought Petty didn't even realize that she was an old age pensioner and he and Danny were still in junior school. She behaved as if they were all the same age. 'What is it, Petty?' he asked, warily. Whenever they got involved with Petty Potts they always seemed to end up uncomfortably close to being dead.

Petty glanced around again. 'I am going away to a conference in Berlin,' she said, in a low voice. 'A very important conference.'

'Are you going to show off your SWITCH spray?' asked Danny.

'No! No! Not yet.' Petty looked quite alarmed. 'The world of science is not ready. I can't reveal my secrets now! Not yet. But—if something were to happen to me . . . ' She peered at them, slowly nodding her head. 'Oh yes—something *could* happen to me, and then my work might never ever be known! And that—*that*—would be a tragedy!'

'Do you think someone's after you then?' whispered Josh.

Petty squinted at him. 'What?'

'You know,' said Josh. 'I mean—you've said before that you think people are spying on you, but do you think they're actually out to get you? Like in films?'

'Good grief, no,' said Petty, as if she thought Josh was simple-minded. 'I just mean that I might get run over by a bus or something. And of course, that could happen at any time! Anyway, just in case it does, while I am away, I want you to keep this!' And she pulled a plastic spray bottle out of her coat; the kind with a squirty button on the top and a little plastic cap over the button.

'We don't want that!' gasped Danny, backing away.

'Oh for heaven's sake! It's perfectly safe—all sealed tight,' said Petty. 'Just pop it under your bed or something and keep it until I get back. Then if I *don't* come back for any reason, you can take it to *New Scientist* magazine and reveal my genius to the world.'

'Petty,' said Josh, 'have you ever noticed that we're not grown-ups? I mean . . . you do realize that we're only eight, don't you?'

'What's that got to do with anything?' said Petty, thrusting the bottle into Josh's hands and then turning and running back down the path. 'See you next week, all being well! Take care, now. And keep searching for the cubes!'

Josh and Danny closed the door and stared at the bottle. 'Wonder which type of spray it is,' muttered Danny. 'Maybe . . . bee or wasp. Or centipede . . .'

'We are not going to find out,' said Josh. Danny nodded. As exciting as their creepy-crawly adventures had been, they had both been nearly eaten far too many times now to want to have a go with Petty's latest spray.

It was still hard to believe, but Petty Potts had created SWITCH spray in the underground lab in her garden, using a secret formula she had worked out during her years with the government in a top secret science department. She might be there still if her so-called friend, the eyebrow-less Victor

Crouch, had not tried to steal her work and then wipe out her memory.

His plan was foiled, though, because Petty had suspected foul play, put a fake formula in her work desk—and hidden the *real* secret SWITCH formula inside six little glass cubes. Then she had recreated it at home when bits of her memory began to come back. It really worked. Josh and Danny ought to know. They'd been SWITCHed four times now.

'Come on,' said Josh, heading up the stairs. 'Let's take this up to our room and find a place to hide it. She's better off not having it, probably. She sprays way too much of this stuff around.'

'We really should just try to stay away from her! Not answer the door next time,' said Danny.

'I know,' said Josh. 'But . . . if we ever *did* find all her other lost secret formula cubes . . . well . . . ' He bit his lip but his eyes shone. Petty had made a second secret formula—to create a spray which could switch them into reptiles—and put it into another six cubes. Only . . . she'd lost them. So far they'd only found four. Without the last two it could never work.

'Imagine,' continued Josh. 'I could be a snake!'

'I could be an alligator!' said Danny.

'*If* we ever find the last two REPTOSWITCH cubes . . . ' sighed Josh. Petty had begged them both to search for her, but who knew where the missing cubes could be? The first four they'd found around the gardens and houses in their neighbourhood, but they might never find the last two. Petty had hidden them too well and that bit of her memory—about where they were—had not come back.

'I could be a giant tree lizard . . . ' went on Danny.

Suddenly something swung down from the top of the banister. 'OI! You little monsters! I knew you'd been messing with my stuff! Gimme my hairspray now!' And Jenny swiped the bottle out of Josh's hands before he could even squeak.

'HEY NO! NO! JENNY, THAT'S NOT YOURS!' shouted Josh. In reply, Jenny just slammed her bedroom door. Josh and Danny stood on the stairs and stared at each other in horror. Then they hurtled up to the landing and across to Jenny's room.

'JENNY! DON'T USE THAT! DON'T SPRAY IT!' they shrieked, in utter panic, crashing her door wide open.

'OUT of my room!' shouted Jenny. She had taken the plastic cap off the spray bottle and was holding it up to her swept-back hair.

'Jenny! Please!' begged Josh, feeling his head reel with panic. 'DO NOT USE THAT SPRAY! It's not what you think it is!'

'Oh ha-ha!' said Jenny. 'Very funny.' And she sprayed a great cloud of SWITCH all over her head.

Fishcakes on Rollerskates

'What are you staring at?' demanded Jenny, slamming the SWITCH spray onto her dressing table as the pale yellow mist settled on her hair and shoulders. 'Get out of my r—'

And then she disappeared.

Danny and Josh stood very still. They didn't dare move. Jenny could be *anything*. And she could be *anywhere*! If she was a fly or an ant she could be right where they might tread if they moved.

'Can you see anything?' whispered Danny, his eyes round and shocked.

'No!' whispered back Josh, desperately scanning the room. He listened for buzzing or chirruping but all he could hear was Piddle the dog barking in the garden and the far-off drone of the vacuum cleaner. Mum was vacuuming the dining room.

'There!' hissed Danny and pointed to the flowery duvet on Jenny's bed. Something was dancing along the yellow flowers. Something which looked confused and panicky. Mind you, this thing *always* looked confused and panicky to Danny. It was a daddy-long-legs.

'A crane fly,' murmured Josh. 'Quick—Danny— shut the door!'

Danny got the door shut in two seconds and then bounded back to the bed to stand next to Josh and stare in wonder at their six-legged sister.

'Wow,' said Danny.

'Yup,' agreed Josh. 'Never expected *this* to happen.'

The crane fly fluttered along the flowery duvet like a nervous and not very talented dancer, jiggling to the left and shimmying to the right and then just clinging to one of the cottony peaks in a shivery way.

'She must be freaking out!' marvelled Danny. 'What should we do?'

'Well,' Josh put his head on one side and considered. 'She's quite safe in here. There are no predators, probably.' He looked at the quivering insect and sighed. 'I suppose one of us ought to spray ourselves and go and look after her. That would be the nice thing to do.'

Danny raised an eyebrow. 'And since when has Jenny ever been nice to *us*?' he asked.

Josh shrugged. 'She is our sister.'

'Right then—off you go!' Danny handed the SWITCH spray to Josh.

'Well—can't we toss a coin or something?' said Josh.

'*You're* the one who wants to be nice!' said Danny.

Josh sighed, took the bottle and sprayed a short
blast on his hand. Any part of the body seemed
to do. 'Just make sure you stay here and don't let
Piddle in—until we're human agai—' he said,
before he too, vanished.

'AAAAAAAAAAAARRRRRRRRRRGGGGGH!'
commented Jenny, as soon as she laid eyes on the
creature frolicking towards her, unaware that it was
her little brother trying to manage more knees than
could ever be right.

'I know what you mean,' said Josh. 'But you
don't look so great, either, Jen!'

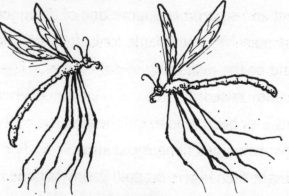

His sister's face was long and horse-like; light
brown, with two thin finger-type things poking
out where her mouth should be. Two short feelers
stuck up from between a pair of eyes which were

large, round, and bulbous and a shimmering
greeny-black colour. Josh was still adjusting to his
own eyes, which gave him a view as if he was
looking through hundreds of tiny lenses all joined
together. He'd had vision like this as an insect
before, so it didn't take him long to get used to
the strange effect—or to the fact that he could see
almost *behind* him with these amazing eyes.

'Josh? Josh?' shrieked Jenny, whirling around in a
circle, her long, elegant brown legs staggering over
the thick tussocks of cotton which tangled across
her duvet. Up this close, the cotton weave looked
like thick woven mesh—the kind of thing you
might see in a metal cable factory. 'Josh?' shrieked
Jenny, again. 'Where are you? Help me! There's a
monster coming for me.'

Josh sighed. 'Jen-eee! I'm he-ere!' he called.

Jenny whirled her long, skinny brown body back
round to face him, screamed loudly, and then fell
into a crumpled heap.

'Oh do stop that!' said Josh. 'Yes—I'm a daddy-
long-legs! So are you! Get over it!'

'How—how—how can I be?' whimpered Jenny.

'It's a long story,' said Josh. 'But don't worry—it *won't last*. It's just for a short while. You'll go back to being normal at any time.'

'My room's g-gone all b-big,' gibbered poor Jenny. 'I don't know what's going on . . . '

Josh frowned. Actually, he couldn't be sure how long Jenny's SWITCHed state would last. He and Danny had only ever had quite short, quick sprays and the effects had lasted about half an hour. The one time they had *drunk* SWITCH, in a special potion form, it had lasted probably ten minutes longer.

But Jenny had really sprayed a gallon of the stuff at her hair, so maybe she'd be a daddy-long-legs for *hours*.

'I—I've got six legs!' she was murmuring now, turning round in slow circles to get a better look at her strange new body. 'And wings. I can fly—sort of. Look!' And she whisked her wings into a thrumming motion and rose up a little way above the duvet like a spindly helicopter. She wasn't very graceful. Her legs dangled about like long socks on a washing line. After a few seconds she flopped back down on the bed. She twitched the strange brown fingery things at her mouth area and stared at Josh. 'I'm dreaming, aren't I?' she said.

'Yes, that's it!' said Josh. 'You are dreaming.' This was *good*, he thought. Jenny really mustn't find out about the SWITCH spray. Far better if she thought she was dreaming. 'Yep—it's all a big mad dream,' went on Josh. 'Do your fishcakes wear rollerskates? Mine do. Eeep.'

Jenny was staring at him as if he'd gone mad.

'It's OK—you're in a dream . . . ? Remember?'
said Josh. 'Being able to fly . . . four extra legs . . .
fishcakes on rollerskates . . . eeep?' Nothing ever
made much sense for very long in *his* dreams.

But Jenny wasn't paying attention. She had
turned away from him and was dragging her flimsy
self across the bed towards the pillow end. She
walked a bit and then rose up and flapped about,
then slumped back down for a while and then walked
a little way again. It was kind of random, thought Josh.
He realized, though, that he was doing the same thing.
'Where are you going, Jenny?' he called after her.

'To explore my dream!' she called back. 'I'm
going *there*!' and she raised one of her forelegs and
waved it towards a huge white edifice, bathed in
glowing golden light. 'I've got to go there!' And
now she took off properly and flew straight towards
the glow.

'Whoa—hang on—wait!' called Josh, taking
off too, to keep up with her. He felt very wobbly in
the air. This was nothing like being a house fly or a
grasshopper. Those creatures had felt like well-oiled

hi-tech machines, swooping through the air and moving around like military aircraft. Being a crane fly was a lot more haphazard. The legs were —well—just stupid! They didn't seem to know what to do with themselves. They wouldn't tuck up neatly under his body, and they didn't work very well when he let them just drop either. They swayed about and messed up his aerodynamics.

Jenny, though, was managing to fly in spite of her legs. She was now zooming straight towards the big golden glow. As he followed his sister, Josh felt the air around him getting warm. There was something he needed to warn Jenny about— something dangerous . . . but oh! The light! The *light*!

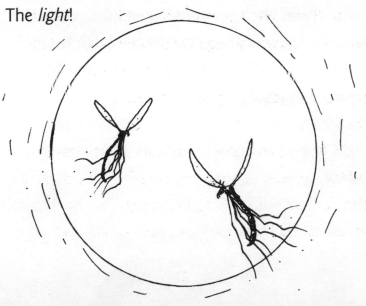

'Isn't it loveleeeeeee?' called back Jenny. 'OW!'
She suddenly jerked backwards as if she'd been
struck. After a confused spiral in the air, she went
towards the light again. 'OW!'

'Oooooooh, the pretty light!' sighed Josh,
zooming towards it. 'OW!' Something hot
smacked him hard in the face. Dazed, he flopped
onto a flat white surface, next to a huge pink spiky
thing. But he didn't stay there long. 'Oooooooh,
the pretty light!' Once again he was up, flying.
'OW!'

'Isn't it loveleeeeeee?' sang Jenny, flapping up
above him. '*OW!*'

Oooh—loveleeee—OW!—oooh—pretty—
OW! It was like a strange song and dance act. He
and Jenny just kept doing it, even though they
didn't know why and even though it hurt, in a
bashy-burny way . . .

They were too mesmerized by the wonderful
light to even notice when one of Jenny's legs
fell off.

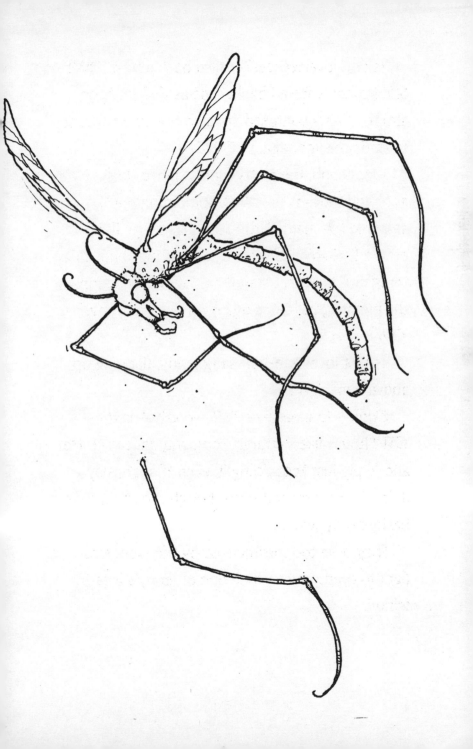

Out on a Limb

Danny had had only seconds to stand gaping at
his transformed brother and sister before Mum
called out 'Danny! Josh!' and began to thud slowly
upstairs, the nozzle of the Hoover making sucky,
thwacky noises against each of the steps as she
worked her way up.

He jumped. Uh-oh! This could be a problem.

'Danny! Josh!' shouted Mum, a bit louder. 'I
want you to go and tidy your room and get the
stuff off the carpet so I can hoover!'

Danny gulped. He looked at the crane flies
skittering about on Jenny's bed and shuddered,
even though he knew they were his brother and
sister. He had to stand here and wait until they got
back safely to human form, so he couldn't answer
Mum and be told to go and tidy his room.

Mum had reached the landing now, lugging

the Hoover up with her by the sound of it. She switched the vacuum cleaner off, sighed, and then called for her sons again. And then she called for Jenny. Nobody answered. Danny stood frozen on Jenny's bedroom carpet, his heart racing. What should he do?

Mum huffed loudly outside Jenny's door and muttered to herself. 'Where have they all gone? Typical, when there's work to be done.'

Then she opened Jenny's door.

She looked around the room, shook her head, and sighed again. Danny stood rigid against the wall behind the door, trying not to breathe. He'd be in big trouble if Mum found out he was hiding and not answering her—but worse, there was no way she'd let him stay in Jenny's room, guarding a couple of daddy-long-legs.

Mum's fingers curled around the edge of the door. She huffed again. And then—mercifully— the door was pulled closed.

Danny sprang towards the bed. He couldn't see the crane flies now. But a buzzy clicking noise told him they were flying against something. Ah! There they were, flapping around the lamp on Jenny's white-painted bedside table.

'Ooh, that's got to hurt,' winced Danny as he saw them ping against the hot bulb and do back flips away from it, rebounding off the inside of the cone-shaped lampshade. 'Josh!' he hissed, aware that Mum was still up on the landing. 'Don't be an idiot. Stop head-butting the light!'

But they kept doing it. Again and again, even though it was clearly hurting them. Danny was about to reach out and switch the lamp off when he saw something shocking on the bedside table, next to Jenny's pink hairbrush. He hoped it was a funny shaped hair—but it was too dark. Jenny's hairs were blonde. This was dark coloured and looked very much like . . .

'A leg!' gasped Danny. 'One of them's lost a leg!'

'Stop! Jenny! Stop!' puffed Josh, lying in a bedraggled heap on her bedside table. 'Look! You've lost a leg!'

He knew it wasn't his leg, as he'd just done a

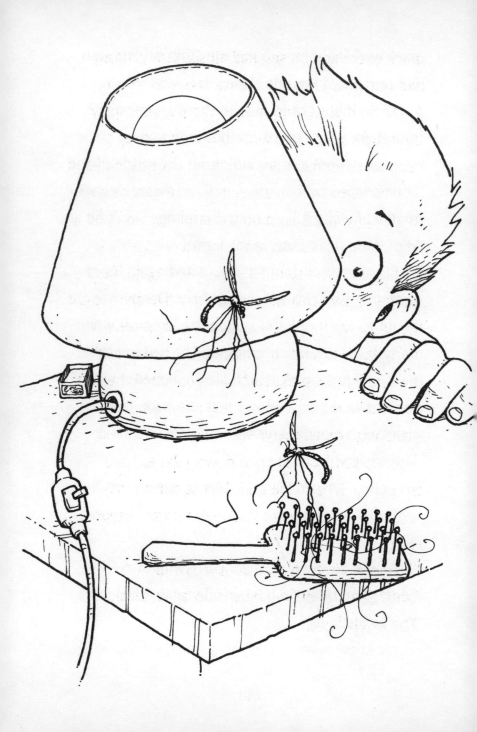

quick check and he still had all six. Jenny, though, had only five. One of her back legs was missing. And here it was, lying next to the big pink spiky thing which Josh had worked out was Jenny's hairbrush. He might not ever have noticed the leg if he hadn't got so exhausted. It was only because he *couldn't* fly at the light now that he had stopped. And resting had given him a moment to realize that he and his sister had gone barmy, just like the moth she'd tried to kill earlier. They had all thought the light was the moon and were instinctively trying to fly towards it, to safety—when in fact it was the bulb in the bedside lamp. Josh's head and feet were very sore with all the burns from smacking against the white hot glass.

Jenny suddenly slapped down next to him, groaning. 'What?' she said. 'What did you say?'

'Look—I don't want you to get upset,' began Josh.

'About what? Hurry up—I've got to fly to the light!' She was pulling herself up again already. 'The lovely light!'

'STOP!' yelled Josh. 'Can't you see that's your bedside lamp? You're just nutting yourself against a white-hot bit of glass!'

'What?' said Jenny, again, but she had flopped down beside him once more.

'And look—you've lost a leg,' said Josh, waving one of his own legs at the poor specimen lying by the hairbrush.

'Ooh,' said Jenny, checking her limbs and noting the stump at the back. 'I *thought* something stung a bit.' She peered at the useless limb.

'Ah well,' said Josh. 'You've got some more.' But he gulped, wondering if he'd switch back and discover Jenny had lost an arm or a leg for good. Why did crane flies have to be so *flimsy*?

At this moment Danny was reaching towards the bedside lamp, carefully avoiding the collapsed crane flies below it, to switch off the tormenting, dangerous light before any more legs fell off. Before he'd reached the switch, the bedroom door, which Mum hadn't properly shut, was suddenly knocked open and in trotted Piddle.

Piddle, a small terrier dog (called Piddle because of an unattractive habit he had when he got over-excited) was very pleased to see Danny. He was bored and wanted to play. He yapped and jumped up on Jenny's bed, even though he wasn't allowed to.

'Piddle! Get out!' hissed Danny. He couldn't shout—Mum was in the bathroom now and might hear him. But Piddle could see that Danny was playing with something. He was pointing his hand at the bedside table. What was going on?

'*OUT!*' hissed Danny, as loudly as he dared.

Piddle heard him. But what he decided Danny was *actually* saying was '*LOOK! LOOK! TAKE A LOOK AT THIS!*'

It's not good, is it?' said Jenny, booting her detached leg about with one of her attached ones. 'I should be bleeding to death.'

'Nah—you're all right,' gulped Josh, trying hard not to think of switching back to Stumpsville. 'Crane flies lose legs like you lose a fingernail. It's a survival thing. If they get caught by a predator they can just shake a leg off and escape.'

'Eurgh,' said Jenny. She examined the stump where her leg had been. It wasn't oozing anything at all. She looked up at the light and sighed longingly.

'NO-OO!' warned Josh. 'Don't fly to the light! You know it doesn't make sense!'

'But . . . ' sighed Jenny. Then she snapped her head round to Josh and said, 'Hang on—predator? You said predator! Are there predators in my dream? I hate dreams like that. I'm going to have to wake myself up if there's a predator after me.'

'We should be OK,' said Josh. 'We're in your bedroom—I don't think there are any big predators there—apart from you. And you're not around.'

Jenny nodded and then froze. Her big bulbous eyes seemed to get even more big and bulbous. A very loud gusty noise suddenly burst into their ears as Jenny stared in horror at something behind Josh. Josh spun round, his legs flapping, and stared too. A huge shadowy figure loomed high into the air—that was probably Danny, Josh told himself. What was far more terrifying was the smaller but still pretty enormous creature which was suddenly springing up and down in front of the bedside table.

A blast of warm air, which smelt of manky old meat, suddenly sent Josh and Jenny flying back towards the big yellow base of the lamp. Jenny screamed. Fair enough, thought Josh, and joined her. 'AAAAAAAAAARGH!' they agreed, as a pair of jaws the size of a tractor snapped shut inches away from them, sending another blast of nasty warm meaty air at them.

'OH NO!' shrieked Josh. 'It's PIDDLE!' He stared at Jenny in horror. 'Piddle EATS creepy-crawlies!'

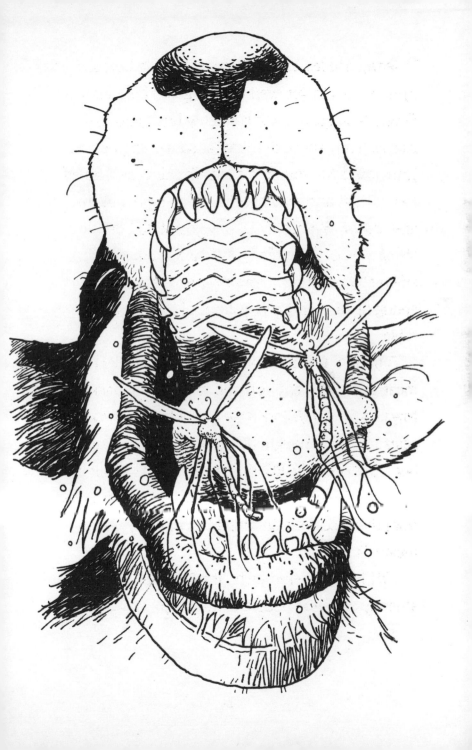

Fetch!

With his front legs Josh grabbed hold of Jenny by the wings and dragged her around to the back of the lampshade. They huddled together on a large plastic tray filled with blue glitter. 'Ooh,' said Jenny. 'I wondered where my eye shadow had gone . . .'

'Jenny!' squawked Josh. 'Don't you think there are more important things to worry about, right now? We're about to be eaten by a giant Piddle!' He cringed back into the corner as a hairy white paw with thick yellow claws suddenly whacked across the table top to their left with a scrunch, and scratched four grooves in the paint. A terrible shrill sound ripped through the air, like a train crashing very fast over and over again. Piddle was yapping. The looming shadow which must be Danny was swooping down on top of Piddle, but would he manage to stop the energetic terrier in time?

'We won't be eaten by Piddle,' said Jenny, quite calmly, even though she was shaking as much as Josh.

'What? How do you know *that*?' gasped Josh, dragging them both further backwards as a smelly pink tongue suddenly shot around the edge of the lamp.

'Because it's *my* dream,' said Jenny, shrugging with all five of her legs. 'And in my dreams, whenever I'm being chased by a monster, it never *actually* gets me. I always wake up just before that happens.'

'B-but . . . ' Josh couldn't think of an answer to this. Telling Jenny this was all *real* probably wouldn't help much.

'Of course *you* might get eaten,' went on Jenny, with a cheerful chuckle. 'You quite often do get eaten or squashed or chucked off a cliff or something, in my dreams. Although Danny is *usually* the first one to cop it. But not me. Nope. In fact, I've had enough of this dream now.' Jenny struggled to stand up straight again. 'I'm just going round to face the monster and then I'll wake up.'

'JENNY! NO!' yelled Josh, horrified, trying to grab her. 'YOU CAN'T! PIDDLE WILL EAT YOU!'

'No he won't—you'll see,' said Jenny, and she fluttered up above him and then scooted round to the front of the lamp again.

'Ee-uw!' she said, as she noticed her discarded leg being licked up by a tongue the size of the kitchen table. The leg disappeared as a shaggy white mouth snapped shut.

'Come on then!' yelled Jenny, bobbing up and down in front of the most terrifying sight she had ever seen (but just not believing it). 'Have another one!'

And she yanked off another leg and threw it in Piddle's face. 'FETCH!' she shouted.

Josh scuttled around the lamp and hid behind the hairbrush. 'JENNY!' he wailed. 'STOP IT! You're going to get EATEN!'

The snappy, yappy jaws were back, wide open, the tongue quivering up and down between sharp yellowy canine teeth. Jenny watched her second leg sail in and the jaws snapped shut. Now she had only four legs left and stood, laughing and bobbing up and down, in the face of doom, looking a bit like a fold-out camping table.

'You want another piece of me?' she yelled. 'See if I care!'

She was looking around and trying to decide which leg to pull off next when Josh made a run for it, grabbed her round her spindly middle and began to drag her away. 'STOP pulling your legs off!' he gasped as she flapped around, angrily. His wings went into overdrive and he managed to drag her up into the air before she could turn herself into a tripod.

'This is *my* dream!' snapped Jenny, struggling hard. 'And I'll pull as many legs off as I *want!* Get out of my dream! You're always coming in and messing with my stuff. I'm telling Mum! Get—'

'—OFF!' yelped Danny and grabbed Piddle by the collar. He yanked the dog away from the bedside table but couldn't see any insect life there at all.

He stared, horrified, into the terrier's mouth. Piddle was panting excitedly, his tail wagging and his tongue lolloping about between his sharp teeth. And on the tongue were a couple of legs. Daddy-long-legs legs. *'Oh no,'* whimpered Danny, 'Josh! Jenny! *Noo!'*

Then a movement caught his eye and he saw a bundle of legs and wings floundering up the wall towards the window. Two crane flies! There were still *two*! The leg count didn't look great for one of them, but they were still alive!

Danny bundled Piddle out of the room and shut the door fast. He lay back against it, his heart thumping in his chest. He'd had such a scare. He'd really thought his dog had just eaten half his family. As he watched Josh and Jenny fluttering along the windowsill, he started to calm down again. He would just sit here, nice and calm, until they popped back up as humans again. That's all. Nothing else.

'Josh? Danny? Jenny? Are you in there?' called Mum, from down in the bathroom. Oh no! She must have heard him shut the door after he'd chucked Piddle out. If she came in now he would never be able to stay and protect Josh and Jenny. Especially if they started that idiotic light-bulb-butting thing again.

Danny looked around him in a panic as Mum switched off the Hoover and stepped out onto the landing. She was heading back to look in Jenny's room again and this time she was suspicious, so she was *sure* to look behind the door.

She would haul him out, tell him off, and send him to his room—and then anything might

happen to Jenny and Josh! Danny gulped as he
heard Mum walk across the landing towards
Jenny's door. Maybe he should just tell her
everything and hope she would believe him
and . . . 'Oh come *on!*' he said to himself, and
then he grabbed the SWITCH spray, dived down
behind the bed and squirted a yellow blast of it
at his head.

The In Crowd

Danny had only just enough time to shove the spray bottle under Jenny's bed before it shot up to the size of a telephone box and the walls and ceiling of Jenny's room rushed away from him, stretching out to the size of a football stadium.

He knew, of course, that nothing had got bigger at all. It was just him—along with Josh and Jenny—who'd got suddenly a lot smaller. Danny stood up carefully, trying to sort out his weird eyes. It was that funny multi-lens thing again. A bit like looking through one of those glass things which gave you loads of the same view in many tiny hexagons. After a few seconds, though, he got used to it and his vision seemed quite normal. He tested out his legs. At least this time—for once—he had *known* what he was going to turn

into before he got sprayed. He tried out his wings
and soon found himself rising up beside the vast
football pitch-sized bed, in a rather wobbly way.

It was nowhere near as good as being a house
fly or a grasshopper. Now, *those* things knew how
to move! Still, it would have to do.

There was a sudden breeze and Danny whirled
round to see the door opening and the humungous
silhouette of what must be his mum. He'd only just
sprayed himself in time! Over on the windowsill,
which now looked like a very wide flat runway on
the edge of a cliff, Danny could see Josh and Jenny,
clinging to the windowpane and bobbing up and
down in that nervous daddy-long-legs way.

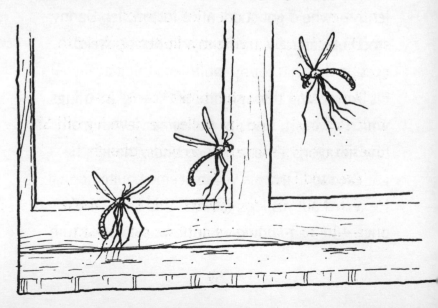

'How are you doing?' he asked, casually, landing behind them. He glanced back into the room but couldn't see Mum now. Maybe she'd gone back out onto the landing

'Danny! What are *you* doing here?' asked Jenny. 'It's bad enough having *one* annoying little brother in my dream, let alone two! I don't get any peace, even while I'm asleep!'

'Hey!' protested Josh, flickering his funny fingery mouth parts. 'I just saved your life!'

'No you didn't!' argued Jenny. 'You just had to interfere! I was going to wake up, if you hadn't come along, but now I'm still in this stupid dream, thanks to you—and now it looks like—' she glared at Danny '—it's just got a lot stupider!'

'Dream?' muttered Danny, fluttering closer to Josh.

'Yep. That's what she thinks this is,' Josh muttered back. 'She just pulled her own leg off! She doesn't think it's anything to worry about . . . '

'Ah,' said Danny.

'What are you doing here?' said Josh. 'You're meant to be guarding us until we get back to normal. And you're not doing a great job of it, are you? Piddle nearly ate us!'

'I know—I'm sorry,' said Danny. 'I shut the door but then Mum came in looking for us and I had to hide, and then she didn't shut the door properly and so Piddle got in. I stopped him! I put him outside again.'

'And you're here now—because?' snapped Josh.

'Because she came in again and I had to shrink down and hide or she'd make me go out. I couldn't guard you then, could I?'

Josh batted his feelers together wearily. 'OK—and—how do you think you can guard us now, Danny? Now that *you* need guarding too!'

'Oh,' said Danny. 'I never thought of that.'

'Ah well,' sighed Josh as Jenny fluttered up and down the windowpane, singing a little song. 'It can't last much longer, anyway. Jenny's got to change back soon. Then I will—and I'll have to guard you until you do. So we must stay safely on the windowsill until then. I just hope the light thing doesn't start up again.' He stared wistfully at the golden glow beside the bed. Danny looked too.

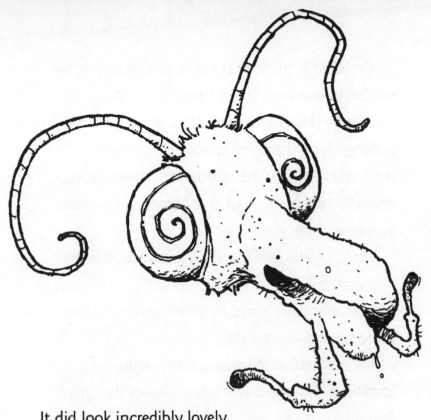

It did look incredibly lovely . . .

'NO!' said Josh, grabbing Danny's wings before
he could take off. 'There's nothing for you there—
except a burnt face!'

Josh and Danny joined Jenny, scuttling up and
down the windowpane, staring through the thick
glass, out into the garden. It was almost dark and
the street lights were coming on. *They* looked nice
too . . . Apart from the tickle-tickle-tickle noises of
their feet on the glass it was all quite peaceful.

'Oh look! It's Chelsea and Louise!' Jenny suddenly squeaked 'Hey! Chelsea! Lou!'

Outside they could see two of Jenny's friends walking along the street towards the house, chatting together. 'Chelsea! Lou!' shouted Jenny, excitedly. 'Up here!' And she flapped her pathetic legs against the glass.

'Erm . . . Jen,' said Josh. 'I don't think they can hear you!'

Suddenly, with a vroom of her spindly wings, Jenny shot up the windowpane and Josh and Danny realized, to their horror, that she was heading for a narrow gap where one of the small top windows was ajar.

'Jenny! NO! Don't go out!' yelled Danny, but it was no good. Jenny wasn't listening and she was already mostly outside, one last leg flicking through after her.

'Oh what?' gasped Josh. 'How did *that* happen? We're meant to be keeping her safe!'

'Quick! After her,' yelled Danny and hurtled up the glass and through the gap after his sister.

The cool evening air was quite refreshing as

Danny and Josh drifted through it, trying to see where Jenny had gone. It smelt of damp grass and late summer blossom. Moths and midges zoomed around them, thrumming and whining.

'There!' said Josh. 'She's down there! Oh no! What does she think she's doing?'

Jenny had always been popular with the girls at school. Somehow, tonight, they weren't so keen. As she glided towards them, calling out their names, the girls at first ignored her. This wasn't so bad.

'It's OK—they're ignoring her,' said Josh. He chuckled. 'She won't like that!'

'Noooo,' said Danny flapping along beside him, and dodging a rather heavyweight moth which was giving him a 'funny look' as it bumbled past. 'Her best mates ignoring her won't do her any harm. It's the bit when they try to kill her which is going to upset her.'

He wasn't wrong. Four seconds later, as Jenny fluttered eagerly in front of Chelsea's nose, a lot of shrieking split the evening air and both Chelsea and Louise began to bash frantically at the creepy leggy thing in their faces.

'EEEEUUUURGH! KILL IT! KILL IT! GET IT OFF ME!' squealed Chelsea.

Poor Jenny did somersaults through the air, horrified. Josh and Danny swooped down and managed to catch her. 'Stop!' yelled Danny as Josh restrained his sister from going back for another try. 'Don't bother, Jen! They're not worth it!'

'I never liked them anyway,' added Josh.

Jenny sniffed. 'I thought they were my *friends*.'

'Yes, but that was before you turned into a four-legged freak,' pointed out Danny.

'And remember,' added Josh. 'This is just a dream, anyway.'

'Ooooooh!' said Jenny and began to flap her way towards something new. She flapped so hard she dragged Josh and Danny with her.

This time it was an *orange* light. A bulb in an orange glass shade, which hung from the wooden beam above a front porch. It was a bit of a jumping, jiving hotspot. It was already heaving with the local nightlife—three large moths were spiralling around inside it, and at least a dozen midges were bouncing up and down in the cooler

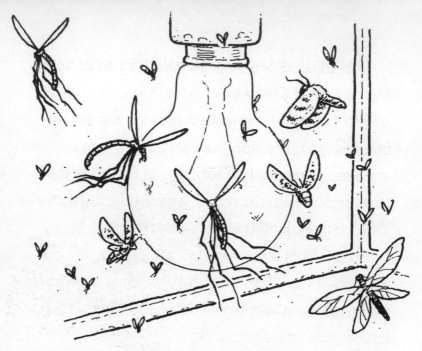

pool of light by the glass rim, while a dozy looking,
see-through lacewing swayed about in one corner,
gazing into a dazzling crystal cube up by the hot
metal bulb socket.

'Oh not *this* again!' moaned Josh as he and
Danny were dragged in with Jenny. 'Jen! You know
you'll only end up getting hurt!'

But Jenny was already head-butting the porch
light and Danny was right up there next to her.
Their cries of delight and pain echoed all around
the orange glass room created by the outdoor
lightshade.

Josh shivered and made himself turn away from the light. The glow was so incredibly tempting! He peered out into the night sky and saw something black and arrow-shaped suddenly zoom past. It made him gulp with horror. He knew what that was. He had seen it circling their garden on many warm summer evenings. It was a bat. A pipistrelle bat. And pipistrelles liked nothing better than a mouthful of crane fly.

Josh took a deep breath and turned round. Ignoring the dozy green lacewing as it fluttered past him into the night air, he dived back into the orange insect disco, and managed to tangle his limbs around Danny and Jenny and tug them back outside. 'There!' he said, pointing a leg at Jenny's bedroom window. 'That's the light we want! That one!' And he zoomed straight for it, dragging his siblings with him.

The dark arrow flitted by so close he heard himself scream. Then he realized it wasn't *his* scream, as the dozy looking lacewing shot over his head, feebly flapping in the vicious teeth of the bat.

Thud-thud-thud. They hit the bedroom window and then Josh dragged Jenny and Danny up to the opening and shoved them through it. Exhausted, they all slid down the inside of the glass and landed in a quivering heap on the sill.

For a few seconds there was peace.

Until . . .

VROOOOOOOOOOOOOOOOOOOOOOOOOOOOOOOOOOOO

'What is THAT?' screamed Jenny.

This Sucks

Josh and Danny stared at each other, mystified. They had heard some weird noises when they'd been shrunk down to creepy-crawlies before, but nothing like this. The howling, droning note just went on and on. And it was getting louder.

'Uh-oh!' gulped Danny, as a gigantic figure loomed back into Jenny's bedroom. It was all too big to take in properly—but he could see a long shining thing, moving in front of the gigantic figure. The long shining thing was making the VROOOOOOOO noise and it was moving from side to side. And getting closer.

'What *is* it?' asked Josh, as Jenny squeaked and shut her wings up tight and scrunched her four legs close together.

'It's Mum,' said Danny. 'And the Hoover.'

'Oh dear,' said Josh.

'Oh help!' yelled Danny. 'It's coming this way.'

And it was. The long shiny thing was waving through the air. Mum always vacuumed the cobwebs off the wall, ceilings, and . . . windowsills!

CRASH!

Suddenly the shiny metal tube, with an enormous round black sucking mouth, was at the far end of the windowsill. A cloud of dust and cobwebs was swirling up in front of it and then being whipped away into the dark tunnel—a tunnel from which there could be no escape.

'FLY! FLY!' shrieked Danny and they all shimmied up into the air, shrieking with fear. The sucking nozzle swept along the sill to the corner where they'd been crouched seconds earlier. Then it began to climb up towards the top corner of the window, where three crane flies were flapping about in a kind of multi-legged disco dance of terror.

'Outside again!' yelled Danny, but Josh saw the black arrow shape flicker past, seeking more insect munchies.

'NO—THIS WAY!' bawled Josh and shot across the glass at an angle, past the upper end of the nozzle. He dropped down as fast as he could go, off the edge of the sill and into a dark narrow chasm.

Plop! Plop! Jenny and Danny skidded in behind him and they all clung to the dusty wallpaper, jiggling up and down with shock. 'We should be safe here,' whispered Josh. 'We're right down behind the radiator.'

'What about spiders?' said Danny, looking around edgily. He'd come horribly close to getting eaten by a spider when he spent some time being a house fly earlier that summer.

'Can't see any,' said Josh.

'OK—what about when she changes back?' said Danny. 'It can't be long now before she cha—I mean, before *she wakes up from her dream*,' he added, realizing that Jenny was listening. 'She's going to end up a bit flat!'

Josh nodded. Changing back to normal would be impossible behind the radiator. Jenny would get squished. She would look like a human waffle.

'Look—I don't know what I'm doing here,' said Jenny, suddenly. 'This is a stupid dream and I've had enough of it. I'm going to meet the sucky monster and get it over with. Then I'll wake up.'

'No! Jenny—don't!' yelled Danny and Josh.

She looked quite surprised. 'You *don't* want me to get sucked up by a monster? Blimey—that's a shock. Well, in that case I'll just have to wake myself up!' She scrunched up her horsey brown face and the little fingery bits on her mouth twiddled through the air as she concentrated hard.

KER-LANGGGGG!
VROOOOOOOOOOOOOOOOOOOO

Josh and Danny and Jenny
all looked up and shrieked. Mum
had changed over to the thin
nozzle—the one that could fit
down behind the radiator
and it was hurtling straight
towards them!

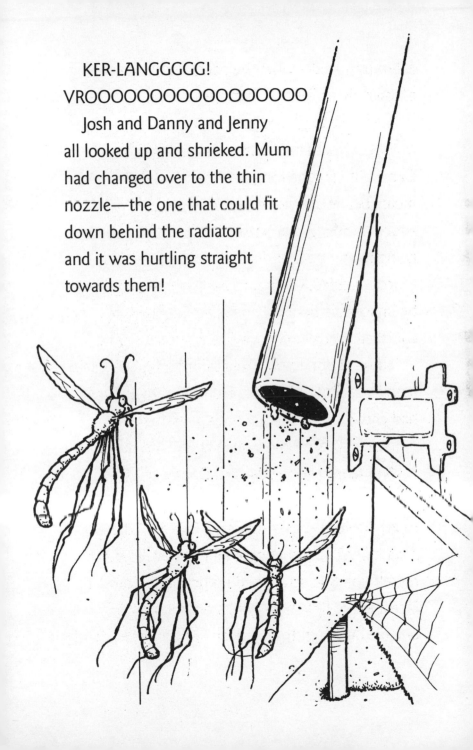

Nozzly Nightmare

Danny went first. He was the closest and suddenly
found his wings were being dragged upwards
by the sucking vortex of air that was funnelling
up into the nozzle. The end of the nozzle was
flattened and narrow, but still wide enough to suck
him right through.

'HEEEEEELP!' he yelled as he tried to hang
on to one of the fixings which held the radiator
to the wall. First his back legs flew up behind
him . . . then the middle ones . . . then . . .

'AAAAAAAAAAAARGH!' he screamed as he lost
his grip and shot up through the air, spinning and
twisting.

'DANEEEE!' shouted Josh, trying vainly to catch
him as he was flung past.

'DANEEEE!' cried Jenny. And she lost her grip

too and was whipped away
up after her little brother.

'NO! JENNY! DANNY!
COME BACK!' wailed Josh,
even as his own back legs
were pulled off the wall
and tugged up, up, to the
swirling black funnel of
death. He could just imagine
spinning and flailing all the
way up the metal nozzle
and along the wobbly plastic
tube into the big chamber
full of dust and fluff and old
crisps and dried up peas and
toenails and dead flies and
dead spiders and dead . . .
he gulped . . . daddy-long-
legs. It was a Hoover tomb.
And he was going into it . . .

THWIP! Up he shot and
had only time to notice
the black rim of the nozzle

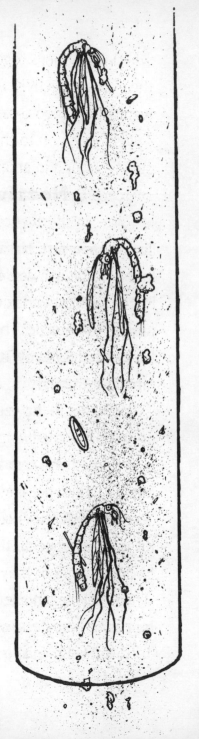

78

whacking his legs together when all of a sudden there was a CLUNK. And the VROOOOOO noise went VROOo-oo-o-sssssssssssssss. And stopped.

Josh clung on to the rim of the narrow nozzle, staring around in amazement. Someone had switched the Hoover off! It was OFF.

Then, in the silence, he heard a whimper. He turned, peering up into the dusty gloom of the nozzle tube and could just make out a tangle of skinny brown limbs and wings and four eyes a little way above him.

'Danny? Jenny?! Are you OK?' he squeaked. They squeaked back. And then they wriggled and a second later they were tumbling down to him. All three of them fell out of the nozzle in a leggy knot and hurtled down to the floor. They didn't have much time to get any of their wings going, but fortunately it was a soft landing. They fell on one of Jenny's slippers.

For a moment they just stared at each other. Then they began the job of untangling and counting limbs. Jenny was sniffing a bit. 'You tried to save me,' she murmured. 'You know, even

though it's just a dream, that was quite sweet of
you both . . . '

Danny and Josh stared at her for a few
astonished moments and then shook their heads
and carried on with the leg sorting.

'How many legs have you lost?' said Danny.

'Two,' said Josh. 'You?'

'One. And a half,' said Danny, inspecting the
one which was snapped off at the knee. 'It does
sting a bit, doesn't it?'

'How about you, Jenny?' asked Josh.

'I feel funny,' said Jenny. She had only three legs
left and her wings were all scrunched up. There
was something about the look on her face which
warned Josh and Danny to back away. Fast.

'Here she goes!' yelled Josh. 'Fly for it!
NOOOW!'

Mum unplugged the Hoover and then wound up
the flex. There was a thud. She turned round and
stared in astonishment at her daughter, who was
lying down next to the radiator, waving her legs in
the air and going, 'One—two! One—two! I've got

two legs! Two legs! Not three! Phew!'

'How did you get down there?' Mum asked,
mystified, not noticing two crane flies which
flapped past her left ear and out onto the landing.

'I don't know,' said Jenny, scratching her head. 'I
think I've been working too hard at school. I've just
had the freakiest dream . . . '

Seeing the Light

Mum looked into Danny and Josh's room. 'Oh! So you're back now, Josh. Where's Danny?'

Josh turned round, with his hands cupped together. 'Oh—he's around,' he smiled, brightly. He seemed quite out of breath.

'What have you got there?' asked Mum, warily. She knew how much Josh loved creepy-crawlies.

'Oh—just a little friend,' said Josh, opening his fingers to reveal a daddy-long-legs with only four and a half limbs.

'He's been through the wars!' said Mum, squinting at Danny.

'Mmmm,' said Josh, giving her a rather hard stare.

As Mum went outside again she heard another thud and grinned, shaking her head. Danny must have been hiding! The boys were playing one of their games.

Danny and Josh ran into Jenny's room.

'Get OUT of my—' began Jenny but they ignored her, dug under the bed and retrieved the SWITCH spray.

'This is our bottle,' said Josh. 'We put water and . . . and . . . '

' . . . Piddle's piddle in it!' added Danny.

'Oooh—you disgusting little . . . ' Jenny tailed
off. She was staring at her bedside lamp in a
dreamy way as Josh ran to put the SWITCH spray
up at the furthest corner of the top shelf of their
highest cupboard.

DINGDONG! chimed the front door. 'Jenny!'
called up Mum. 'It's Chelsea and Louise!'

Danny and Josh sat at the top of the stairs and
watched Jenny walk down. Chelsea and Louise
stood by the door. 'Hi!' they both called. 'You want
to come out?'

Jenny stared at them through narrow eyes, her
arms folded.

'Come on,' laughed Chelsea. 'What are you looking all funny about? You wait till you hear what we've heard about Kelly Smith! You'll just *die*!'

'Yes. I might just do that,' snapped Jenny. 'You know . . . I don't think I do want to come out with you tonight. The pair of you—you just *kill* me!'

Chelsea and Louise stared at Jenny and then at each other, as she propelled them back outside.

'OK—don't get in a flap, Jen,' giggled Chelsea. 'Come on out! Just as you are. You look great in that short skirt. All leggy!'

Jenny stared at her legs and then glared at Chelsea. 'Just don't fancy the disco tonight,' she growled.

'So—what—you're just going to sit at home all evening?' gasped Louise, astonished.

'Yes,' said Jenny. 'I'll see you tomorrow. But tonight, for some reason, I just want to look at my bedside lamp.'

She didn't even notice Josh and Danny rolling about laughing on the landing as she stomped back upstairs.

Shady Secret

'Here! Take it back!' said Danny, as soon as Petty opened her front door. He thrust the spray bottle into her hand and she scowled and pulled them quickly into her hallway, slamming the door shut behind them.

'Have you forgotten *everything* I've told you?' she demanded. 'Remember—we may be being watched! At any time! I told you, there are government spies always keeping me under surveillance.'

Josh folded his arms. 'But if this Victor Crouch guy *really* burnt out your memory and got you kicked out of the government's secret science labs, why would they bother with you again? They must think you don't know anything.'

'You really don't pay attention, do you?' snapped

Petty. 'Victor Crouch realized—too late—that the research he stole from me was fake! He will not have been able to make SWITCH spray himself, because the code for making it is here, with me! And all *he* got was the *fake* code.

'So he will be having me watched, just in case I look like I might be able to remember again. He's hoping I'll still be active.'

'Active?' echoed Danny.

'Yesss! Working as a genius scientist once more. Which, of course, I am! But nobody knows it except me and you. So that's why we have to be careful. I have to carry on looking like a scatterbrained old biddy. And *you* have to carry on looking for the missing REPTOSWITCH cubes, if we're ever going to make the reptile spray. I don't suppose you've found another one, have you?'

Petty wandered into her kitchen and took two small velvet boxes off a high shelf. She opened the red one to reveal six sparkling glass cubes, each with a tiny hologram inside it. These were BUGSWITCH cubes, each containing a vital part of the code for making BUGSWITCH spray.

Petty smiled and ran her fingertips over the six cubes. Then she opened the green velvet box, revealing only four cubes in a tray meant for six.

There had been only one cube when Josh and Danny first saw the box. They had managed to find three of the missing ones. 'I tried to work out the code with just these four cubes last week,' Petty said. 'I thought I might be able to remember the missing parts—but I can't. If you two can't find the last two cubes, I might as well give up.'

'Well, we are trying, you know,' said Danny.
'When we're not having to deal with the trouble
your SWITCH spray keeps making for us! Did
you know that our *sister* was SWITCHed on
Wednesday?!'

Petty dropped onto a kitchen chair, shocked.
'No!'

Josh and Danny told her what had happened.
'But you don't have to worry,' said Josh, at the end
of their story. 'She thinks it was all a dream.'

Petty sighed and took her spectacles off. 'I
think I'm going to have to lie down under a damp
flannel,' she said. 'Come on—better go home now,
boys. Sorry about your sister.'

As she shooed them onto the front step, Danny
glanced up. 'Hey!' he said. 'That was the little
orange room we flew into! We were up in there,
head-butting your light!'

They all stared up into the porch lightshade
and then Josh squinted. 'Wait a minute,' he said.
'Petty—can you get me a chair?'

'Whatever for?' snapped Petty.

'I remember seeing something up in that light

. . . something strange . . . ' Josh screwed up his eyes. Yes . . . there was a strange little sparkle of light up inside the glass shade.

Petty brought out a chair and Josh stood on it. Reaching up, on his tiptoes, he put his hand into the shade. Two dead moths fell out and Danny gave a little shriek. 'Well . . . ' he said. 'I *met* them a couple of nights ago!'

Josh stepped back off the chair with something in his hand. He smiled at Petty and opened his fingers. In his palm lay a glass cube, with the hologram of a gecko inside it.

'REPTOSWITCH cube, anyone?' said Josh.

DIARY ENTRY *612.3

SUBJECT: FIVE REPTOSWITCH CUBES!!!

Hurrah! Getting Josh and Danny into the project paid off again today. They had another SWITCH adventure and ended up in my porch light—where it turns out I had hidden the fifth REPTOSWITCH cube!

It is a bit worrying that their sister got caught up in things and was also turned into a crane fly, but both boys insist that she still thinks it was only some kind of weird dream.

Another worry are the flashes of light. I have seen them several times now—in the trees at the park, and in the hedges opposite my house. I was certain I saw a flash when Josh got up on the chair and pulled the REPTOSWITCH cube out of the porch light.

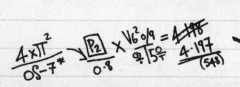

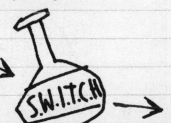

It could just be an old broken bottle reflecting the sun . . . or it could be someone spying on me through binoculars. Victor Crouch's spies could be anywhere! I keep imagining that old eyebrow-less freak staring through my windows . . .

But I suppose I do have to remember that sometimes I see and hear things which aren't really there. That's all part of the package when you're a genius. I will make sure Josh and Danny keep very watchful, though.

Just in case.

But when we find the last cube, I can start trying out REPTOSWITCH spray on them! And if I can persuade them to be an alligator for an hour or two . . . perhaps I can also persuade them to snack on Victor Crouch!!!

Ah ha! Ah ha ha ha ha! Erm. Scary powerful laugh etc. (It doesn't really work, written down, does it?)

<u>REMEMBER</u>

PLACES TO VISIT

Want to brush up on your bug knowledge?
Here's a list of places with special areas dedicated
to creepy-crawlies.

Liverpool Museum
http://www.liverpoolmuseums.org.uk/wml/
naturalworld/bughouse/

Marwell Wildlife Park
http://www.marwell.org.uk/

Natural History Museum
http://www.nhm.ac.uk/

Remember, you don't need
to go far to find your favourite
bugs. Why not venture out
into your garden or the
park and see how many
different creatures
you can spot.

WEBSITES

Find out more about nature and wildlife
using the websites below.

http://www.bbc.co.uk/cbbc/wild/

http://www.nhm.ac.uk/kids-only/

http://kids.nationalgeographic.com/

http://www.switch-books.co.uk/

Another exciting adventure awaits . . .

Ali Sparkes
Winner of the Blue Peter
Book of the Year

Illustrated by
Ross Collins

S.W.I.T.C.H.

SERUM WHICH INSTIGATES TOTAL CELLULAR HIJACK

Beetle Blast

Let Them Eat Cake

By the time the toxic cloud reached him it was already too late. Josh went cross-eyed, grabbed his throat and gurgled. He slumped onto the bed, his face going purple.

'Mmm—mmm—muuu,' he rasped.

His poisoner stood over him, smirking; immune to the gas.

'Muuu—' gasped Josh, falling off the bed and crawling towards the door. 'MUM! Danny's guffing at me again!'

Danny grinned proudly as his twin brother fell out onto the landing, sucking in grateful breaths of clean air.

Mum was less amused. She put her head round their bedroom door and then withdrew it again, smartish.

'Danny! That's revolting! Go to the toilet at once!' she called from the other side of the door. 'Good grief! What is going on in your innards?'

'It's you that feeds me,' pointed out Danny.

'Don't be cheeky!' snapped Mum.

'It's OK—I've stopped now,' said Danny, stepping out to see his twin slumped against the banisters, flapping a hand in front of his face.

'Well I hope so!' said Mum. 'I don't want you embarrassing Josh at the Wild Things meeting.'

Danny blinked in surprise. 'Wild Things? I don't go to Wild Things! *I'm* not the freaky little bug boffin. That's just Josh!'

Josh might be identical to Danny on the outside (although a lot less fluffy on the hair front and without the skater-boy clothes) but on the inside the brothers couldn't have been more different, thought Danny. He loved loud music and skateboarding and kicking footballs around, while Josh loved peering at nature through a magnifying glass. That's why he'd signed up for Wild Things and had started to go every week, with a load of other freaky little bug boffins. Danny had no intention of joining him!

'I'm sorry, but you *have* to go,' said Mum, taking some towels into the bathroom. 'Your football coach rang to say practice is cancelled and I'm going to pick up my new car, so there's nobody to look after you. You're going with Josh.'

'Oh *no*!' wailed Josh. 'He's going to guff all the way through!'

'Ah well,' sighed Danny. 'I'll just have to set up my own Wild Things gang—the Stink Bugs.'

'Just *try* to act interested,' hissed Josh as he and Danny joined the other Wild Things at

the Blackthorn Wildlife Centre. They met every
Monday after school to do experiments and nature
trails and look at things through microscopes.
Today they were going pond dipping to see what
they could find.

'Danny, meet Ollie, Milo, Biff, and Poppy,' said
Josh, pointing to each of his fellow bug boffins
in turn. They all wore 'nature freak' clothes,
Danny noticed. Lots of green and brown and little
sleeveless jackets with loads of pockets—just
like Josh. Danny, in his bright orange sweatshirt
and baseball cap, looked like a traffic cone by a
hedgerow.

'Hi, Danny,' said Biff, who had a pair of
binoculars round his neck.

'Greetings,' said Ollie and Milo, together. They
both had spectacles and funny green hats, like
pensioners wore in the garden.

'Hi, Danny, nithe to meet you,' lisped Poppy,
who had brown plaits, freckles, and a rather
alarming number of teeth. She rattled a little plastic
tub at him and whispered, 'Antth' eggths!' with
her eyebrows going up and down.

'Er . . . yeah,' said Danny, backing away.

'Look—Grandadth come to help today,' said
Poppy, pointing to a tall man in a low-brimmed
hat who was standing nearby, gazing out of the
window. Danny noticed he had a strange, black,
pointed fingernail on the little finger of his left
hand. Well, weirdness obviously ran in the family.

'I think she likes you,' sniggered Josh, as Poppy
smiled scarily at Danny and stroked the lid of her
plastic tub. 'She wants to take you home . . . '

'Shut up!' hissed Danny, and hurried away
towards some interesting buttons near a collection
of wildlife pictures. They made wildlife-y noises

when he pressed them. *Ribbit.* 'Toad,' said Danny. *Chirrup.* 'Grasshopper,' said Danny. *Zzzzzzz.* 'Bluebottle.'

'See,' said Josh. 'You're quite good at this stuff.'

'Only because . . . ' said Danny, ' . . . *we've* either been one of them or nearly been *eaten* by one of them.'

'Shhhh!' hissed Josh, looking around uneasily. 'Don't tell everyone!'

'What? That our mad next-door-neighbour keeps turning us into creepy-crawlies?' said Danny, making no effort at all to be quiet. 'Yeah, right. Everyone's going to believe *that*!'

Someone poked Danny hard in the ribs and went 'Shhhhh, you numbskull! You never know who might be listening! And I am *not* mad. I am a genius!'

Danny and Josh spun round, gaping with shock. There stood Petty Potts, the old lady from next door. In her tweedy hat and glasses, carrying a straw bag and smiling sweetly, you would never guess what she truly was—a brilliant scientist with a secret laboratory hidden beneath her

garden shed. Earlier that year Josh and Danny had stumbled into it while she was in the middle of one of her astonishing experiments—to change things into creepy-crawlies.

They had got caught up in a jet of her SWITCH spray and shortly afterwards morphed into spiders. Which was a bit of a shock. It was a small miracle that they hadn't been squashed flat, drowned, or eaten. And since then, despite trying really hard to steer clear of any further spraying, they had each been turned into a bluebottle, a grasshopper, an ant, and a daddy-long-legs. Thankfully, only temporarily.

'What are *you* doing here?' spluttered Josh.

'It's a free country!' said Petty. 'I'm allowed into my local wildlife centre, aren't I?'

Danny eyed her bag nervously, looking for the telltale plastic spray bottle.

'You needn't look so petrified, Danny!' she said. 'I haven't got any SWITCH spray with me today.'

Danny sighed with relief. It wasn't so much the 'being a creepy-crawly' he minded—more the 'nearly being eaten' so very often. He'd also once spent more time than he wanted to remember hiding in a cat's ear while he was a grasshopper. And he was haunted still by the things he'd eaten when he was a bluebottle.

'No,' said Petty, reaching into her bag and pulling out a small tin. 'No spray today. This time it's in pellet form. I want to SWITCH a rat. I need to try out more mammals—other than you two. I'm going to hide the pellets in some food!' She leaned in towards them and whispered, 'Don't forget to keep looking out for the REPTOSWITCH cube! Only one more to find.' She looked edgily around her. 'And never forget you might be being

watched! Victor Crouch's people are everywhere!'
And she strode off, before Danny or Josh could say
anything else.

Josh shrugged. 'Well, at least there's no chance
we'll get caught out by *pellets*,' he said. 'Let's just
pretend we don't know her.'

'She's never going to let up about that blinkin'
cube, is she?' muttered Danny. 'We've found four
of them and she already had one—you'd think
she'd be happy with that!'

'Yes—but without the *last* cube, she can't work
out the REPTOSWITCH code, can she?' said Josh.
'And without the code she'll never be able to
make the spray and we'll never get a chance to be
alligators or snakes.'

Josh and Danny looked at each other and
bit their identical lips. Although most of their
adventures as creepy-crawlies had been terrifying,
they'd also been exciting and, at times, quite
brilliant. Both boys knew how it felt to fly, to leap
twenty times their own body-length, to run up
walls, and walk upside down along ceilings. It was
just the nearly getting killed . . .

But being a reptile would be different! Most reptiles were tough and much, much bigger than a creepy-crawly. It would be amazing to become a big scaly predator! That was why they had agreed to help Petty find her missing cubes, so she could crack the REPTOSWITCH code.

'Come on,' said Josh. 'We're not going to worry about the last cube here. She's hardly going to have hidden it half a mile from her house.'

'We're not going to worry about being watched by government spies, either,' grinned Danny. 'All that "*Victor Crouch is after me*" business! *That's* all in her head!'

The Wild Things went to scoop creatures out of the pond. Danny mooched along after them, bored and trying not to notice Poppy smiling and waving at him with her little glass jar on a bit of pink string. He did *not* want to get to know a dragonfly nymph or a newt—or Poppy. It was a stupid waste of time. He sat down at a picnic bench while the others squelched about by the edge of the water, ooohing and aaahing about tiny splodgy brown life-forms.

Danny's stomach rumbled. He noticed a plate left on the table. On it was a sticky chocolate muffin bought from the wildlife centre café. With just a bit broken off. A rich sweet chocolatey smell was wafting across from it. Danny's mouth watered. He looked around to see if anyone was coming to claim it. Nobody seemed to be. He peered at it a little closer. No wasps on it.

Another chocolatey waft reached him. Danny couldn't resist. He grabbed the abandoned cake and bit into it. 'Mmmmm-mmmm,' he groaned, happily.

'Danny! Come and see this!' said Josh, crouching in some bog weed. The other Wild Things had wandered off to the other end of the c-shaped pond, and were on the far side of some bushes. Danny felt he could bear to show some interest with Poppy no longer goggling at him.

He took the muffin with him and ambled over.

'See!' said Josh, pointing at a muddy pebble. 'A great crested newt!'

'Hey. Wow.' Danny shrugged.

'What are you eating?' asked Josh, sniffing at his brother.

'Muffin. 'ave some,' said Danny, handing the last chunk to his brother.

Josh held up his muddy hands. 'Stick it in for me, will you?' he said, opening his mouth. Danny shoved it in.

'Mmm, nice chunky chocolate drops,' mumbled Josh.

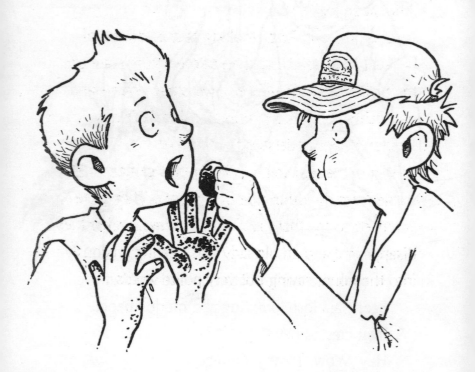

'Hey!' said a sharp voice behind them. 'Who's had my cake?'

Danny spun round, guiltily. Standing by the picnic bench was . . . oh *no* . . . Petty Potts.

Petty stared at him and then at Josh, who had turned round too. 'Oh dear, oh dear, oh dear,' she said, spotting the chocolate crumbs around their mouths.

'What *kind* of oh dear?' asked Josh, sounding a little bit squeaky.

'Ummm,' said Petty, looking at the little tin of pellets in her hand and then at the empty plate on the picnic table. There were two small pops—and no further point in explaining. Josh and Danny wouldn't have understood.

When the remaining Wild Things came round from the other side of the pond, they were surprised to see that Josh and his bored brother had disappeared and an old lady was peering anxiously into the pond, saying not very polite words.

FUN AND GAMES

There are more games for you to play and
download free on the S.W.I.T.C.H. website.
www.switch-books.co.uk

Word search

Search for the hidden words listed below:

PIDDLE	HOOVER
JENNY	LAMP
LIGHT	JOSH
CRANE FLY	DANNY
LACEWING	BAT

P	I	D	D	L	E	H	H	M	S
M	B	I	V	E	S	T	G	A	N
A	C	H	O	O	T	H	N	L	I
L	W	R	J	T	U	C	I	Y	D
F	S	D	A	N	N	Y	W	L	E
J	K	B	L	N	A	N	E	J	O
U	E	T	E	R	E	I	C	E	U
R	E	V	O	O	H	F	A	N	J
S	K	S	T	H	G	I	L	N	C
X	H	M	C	L	R	T	B	Y	P

Answers on page 122

Spot the difference

These pictures *look* the same, but can you spot ten differences?

Answers on page 122

Are you a bug boffin?

Question 1)
PETTY LEAVES HER SWITCH SPRAY
WITH THE BOYS WHILE SHE GOES
AWAY, BUT WHERE IS SHE GOING?
A) Back to her lab to work on her
SWITCH formula
B) To the park to try out her
SWITCH spray on some squirrels
C) To a conference in Berlin

Question 2)
HOW MANY LEGS DOES JENNY LOSE
WHILE SHE IS A CRANE FLY?
A) 3
B) 4
C) 2

Question 3)
WHAT REASON DOES JOSH GIVE FOR
CRANE FLIES LOSING THEIR LEGS SO
EASILY?
A) Crane flies are clumsy and often
break off their legs by accident
B) It's a survival tactic for escaping
predators
C) Crane flies shed their legs each
summer and they grow back

Question 4)
WHY ISN'T JENNY SCARED WHEN
PIDDLE TRIES TO EAT HER?
A) She thinks Piddle is just trying
to be friendly
B) Jenny is too distracted by the
lampshade to worry about Piddle
C) She thinks it's all a dream

Question 5)
WHAT ARE JENNY'S FRIENDS
CALLED?
A) Chelsea and Louise
B) Natalie and Charlotte
C) Lola and Catherine

Question 6)
HOW MANY REPTOSWITCH CUBES
HAVE JOSH AND DANNY COLLECTED
BY THE END OF THE STORY?
A) 4
B) 5
C) 3

Question 7)
WHERE DO JOSH AND DANNY FIND
THE LATEST REPTOSWITCH CUBE?
A) Behind the radiator in Jenny's
bedroom
B) Underneath Jenny's bed
C) Inside Petty Potts's porch light

Question 8)
WHAT ARE CRANE FLIES ALSO
KNOWN AS?
A) Mummy-longer legs
B) Daddy-long legs
C) Dingly-dangly legs

Answers on page 123

Missing pieces

Can you work out which piece of the puzzle is missing?

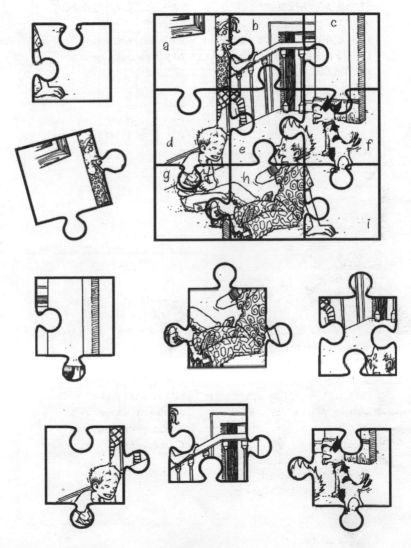

Answer on page 123

Answers

Word search (page 118)

P	I	D	D	L	E	H	H	M	S
M	B	I	V	E	S	T	G	A	N
A	C	H	O	O	T	H	N	L	I
L	W	R	J	T	U	C	I	Y	D
F	S	D	A	N	N	Y	W	L	E
J	K	B	L	N	A	N	E	J	O
U	E	T	E	R	E	I	C	E	U
R	E	V	O	O	H	F	A	N	J
S	K	S	T	H	G	I	L	N	C
X	H	M	C	L	R	T	B	Y	P

Spot the difference
(page 119)

Answers

Are you a bug boffin?
(page 120)

Answer 1) C

Answer 2) A

Answer 3) B

Answer 4) C

Answer 5) A

Answer 6) B

Answer 7) C

Answer 8) B

Give yourself a point for every question you got right.

6–8 POINTS — You are a real bug boffin! Nothing gets past you.

3–5 POINTS — You are SWITCHed on! You enjoy a good adventure.

0–2 POINTS — Oh dear, looks as if you need to brush up on your bug skills! Better luck next time!

Missing pieces
(page 121)

g

About the author

Ali Sparkes grew up in the woods of Hampshire.
Actually, strictly speaking she grew up in a house
in Hampshire. The woods were great but lacked
basic facilities like sofas and a well stocked fridge.
Nevertheless, the woods were where she and
her friends spent much of their time and so Ali
grew up with a deep and abiding love of wildlife.
If you ever see Ali with a large garden spider on
her shoulder she will most likely be screeching
'AAAAAAAAAARRRRRGHGETITOFFME!'

Ali lives in Southampton with her husband and sons
and would never kill a creepy-crawly of any kind. They
are more scared of her than she is of them. (Creepy-
crawlies, not her husband and sons.)

Other books
in the S.W.I.T.C.H. series
SERUM WHICH INSTIGATES TOTAL CELLULAR HIJACK

Spider Stampede

Fly Frenzy

Grasshopper Glitch

Ant Attack

Beetle Blast